The Lost Nickel

Zachary Williams

NEIGHBORHOOD READERS

Rosen Classroom Books & Materials™

New York

Where is my nickel?

Is it on my bed? No.

Is it on my table? No.

Is it in my bag? No.

Is it in my hat? No.

Is it in my jar? No.

Here it is.
It is in my pocket!